gaze of GRACE

Some gazes don't just see you,
they change you.

DRAB TOAD

Published by Notion Press - February 2025
ISBN: 979-8897244546

This book is a work of fiction inspired by lived emotion. Names, characters, timelines, and events have been changed, blended, or imagined for storytelling purposes. Any resemblance to real people or situations is coincidental.

Nothing in these pages is meant to harm, expose, or target anyone. It's just a story, written honestly, imperfectly, and as it came.

Some things stay unspoken,
not because they're small, but because they matter
too much to say out loud.

Table of Contents

I didn't write this because I wanted to.
I wrote it because it wouldn't leave me alone.

Some memories sit silent until one day they don't,
and suddenly you're writing about things you thought
you buried.

I'm not here to teach, preach, or explain.
I'm just telling a story the way it happened,
messy, soft, slow, sometimes contradictory.

You don't have to agree with it.
Just walk with it.

And if you're carrying something unsaid,
maybe this book won't fix it,
but maybe it'll make you feel less alone while you hold
it.

Read at your pace.

— Author.

What truly begins a story, the moment it happened, or the moment we finally admit it mattered?

Not everything starts with impact.
Some things begin silently,
like a shift in someone's voice,
a look held one second too long,
a memory that refuses to stay where it was put.

This isn't a story of perfect people.
It's just two humans trying to understand themselves
in the presence of someone who sees too much.

There are no heroes here.
No clean lessons.

Just moments.
Some small.
Some heavy.
Some that changed everything
without announcing themselves.

If you stay long enough,
you'll see what they couldn't say out loud
while living it.

CHAPTER 01

The Gravity of Her Gaze

*Some encounters don't knock,
they shift the ground, change the map inside you,
before you even understand what moved.*

Not all turning points announce themselves. Some slip in between minutes, dressed in routine. You mistake them for nothing, until they start to reshape you.

This isn't a story that begins with certainty. It starts like a door nudged open by wind: unplanned, accidental, irreversible.

Between syllabus and schedule, where no one's name yet matters, something older stirs. It's not love… not yet. It's the rearranging of your world when a stranger's pattern interrupts your own.

So, we begin. Not in noise or narrative, but in the gravity of a gaze that didn't ask to be remembered, yet somehow was.

What follows isn't a love story. It's the slow undoing of a pattern. The first awareness that maybe one day, love will need to be written in.

The campus was finally awake again.
After weeks of silence, it sounded like itself... loud, restless, alive. Students filled the corridors, talking over each other, trying to find the pulse of being back.

Aryan stepped out of the lecture hall like he always did. Slow. Unbothered. Wearing that half-lost look people wear when nothing feels urgent. His bag hung from one shoulder. No hurry. Just another day.

Then he heard footsteps.
Quick. Uneven. Not like the rest.

He looked up without really meaning to.

At the top of the stairs. She appeared.

Not dramatically. Just... there. But something about that small moment hit different. Like the air shifted a little.

She didn't stand out in any obvious way. No loud clothes, no big entrance. But the way she moved: calm, natural. Like water finding its path. It made everything else blur for a second.

Aryan didn't know her. He didn't even know why he noticed her. But something in him stopped moving.

Sara.

She laughed at something her friend said. It wasn't a loud laugh. It was soft, easy, like she didn't care who was listening.

And then her eyes met his.

Not for long. Not even enough to call it a moment. But it happened. A quick spark, a connection so brief it almost didn't exist.

Still, it did. And it stayed.

He didn't move. He didn't even blink for a second.
And just like that, she looked away.
Walked down the stairs.
Gone.

The crowd swallowed her up like it always does. But Aryan stood there, frozen in the middle of noise.

Something small had shifted. He didn't know what, or why. But it felt like something inside him had been tapped on the shoulder. Something that had been asleep for a while.

He kept watching the space she had just walked through. Trying to catch it again. That feeling. That jolt you don't know what to do with.

He let out a slow breath. Half a sigh. Half a question.

"What the hell was that?"

The campus went on around him. People talking, laughing, rushing to class. But he didn't move.

As if some invisible mark had been left on him.
And now, no matter how hard he tried, part of him was already looking for her again.

THE UNASKED FOR

She wasn't just someone he saw.
She was a stop in the stream of his day,
a pause that didn't ask for attention,
an answer to a question
he hadn't known was waiting.

Her laugh didn't ring out.
It stayed with him,
like a low note that stays in the air
after the music ends.

And in that one small moment,
she wasn't a mystery to figure out.
She was something to keep close,
like a smooth stone in his pocket,
a small weight
to remember her by.

CHAPTER 02

The Second Glance Holds

Some people move like time owes them patience.
She was one of them.

It's a boy-sees-girl moment. A spark, a glance, a disruption. Sometimes someone awakens a forgotten room within you. It isn't loud or lustful; it's foundational. This isn't about fate written in stars or love at first sight. It's about connection without conversation, longing without pain.

A reminder that the world changes not through explosions, but through unnoticed arrivals. And how sometimes, the people who move us most barely speak.

In the smallest of exchanges, the seeds of something greater are sown. Sometimes, it doesn't take much. Just a glance that remembers you.

It had been days since that brief encounter on the stairway. Nothing that ought to have stayed. But it did. Not like a wound or a wildfire, more like a song in the background. Soft, constant, unshakable. Something unfinished, not urgent, but still there.

And now, here she was again.

The elective class had a different pace from the regular ones. Looser, slower, people wandering in from different departments, carrying their half-awake energy. Aryan wasn't really paying attention until his name was called and paired with hers.

He looked up, almost on instinct.

Sara.

Two rows ahead, she turned. This time their eyes didn't just brush, they stayed. There was something in it. Not intensity, not recognition, just a soft crossing. Then she smiled, quick, easy, like an inside joke with the universe.

"So, Mr. Perfectionist," she said as she slid into the seat beside him. "How do we start?"

Aryan leaned back, folding his arms. "Maybe by showing up? Unlike your grand plan to disappear today."

She laughed, mock-offended.
"You were eavesdropping? Rude."

He didn't plan to smile, but he did.

They worked together through the assignment. Her comments light and teasing, his replies measured but sharp-edged. Sara had a kind of presence that didn't need space cleared for it. It simply stayed. She tapped her pen as she thought, a small habit that matched her calm. And when she smiled fully, a dimple appeared, brief but certain.

Aryan wasn't in the habit of noticing details. But he did.

She caught him watching.
"What?"
"Nothing," he said, looking back at the page.
She let it go, but her eyes told him she'd noticed more than he admitted.

Before meaning is born, there's observation. Aryan didn't rush to understand her. He just noticed: the way she moved, the soft consistency in how she showed up, the way her presence didn't ask for attention but always found it anyway. And she, though she said nothing, sensed it too. Something unspoken forming between them. Not a spark. Not a reveal. Just awareness.

The class passed too quickly. As they packed up, Sara slung her bag over her shoulder.
"Same time next week?"
"Same time," Aryan said. His voice carried a certainty he hadn't planned.

She walked away; her laugh left behind like a thread in motion. Aryan stayed seated a little longer than he needed to. It wasn't infatuation, or even clarity. It was something softer, and somehow more real. Not an emotion. Not a moment of change. Just something that stayed.

Some moments don't create connection.
They reconnect you. To something ancient you never got to finish.

THE TANGLE

Her laugh stayed behind,
soft and sure,
a single note finding its home.

He looked away,
something in him softening.
The moment was too full for words.

If life moves in circles,
this was no meeting,
just two paths
touching in the dark.

What tied them then?
No one.
Just a thin thread
drawn between them
without a sound.

Not every turning point needs to
announce itself.
Some arrive in small moments,
a glance held,
a name spoken aloud
for the first time.

The foundation of something
meaningful is often built
where we least expect it,
between laughter and silence,
between showing up and staying.

Let this be a reminder:
even beginnings that feel like chance have
their own weight.

CHAPTER 03

Where Silence Begins to Speak

Before words find meaning, there's a calm space where presence begins to do the talking. Not every connection moves through expression; some deepen in what's left unsaid. After the first spark fades, what remains is the slower current of understanding: less visible, but more real.

This is where Aryan and Sara begin to meet differently, not through conversation or curiosity, but through the spaces that ask for nothing and still reveal everything.

Here, silence isn't absence.

It's awareness taking shape.

Some silences don't end the conversation.
They deepen it.

SEEING HER SILENCE
Some people don't need to speak to fill a room. She was one of them. What Sara carried wasn't

absence: it was a kind of calm that shaped the air around her, constant and alive, the kind that doesn't shrink or shout.

There are people who don't fight the distractions of the world; they simply make them fade. When she sat there, the world didn't stop. It adjusted, as if something in it wanted to listen better.

Aryan didn't notice her because she was distant; he noticed her because her presence had weight, even when it asked for nothing. It wasn't mystery, and it wasn't performance. It was presence that didn't falter under attention, silence that held its own truth.

And in seeing that, something in him softened. He didn't know what to name it yet, but he knew it wasn't leaving anytime soon.

The classroom moved like time forgotten. Not in speed, but in absence. The atmosphere was dull and familiar: faint lectures fading mid-air, pens moving more from obligation than belief, a chair creaking against its own weight. Behind all that noise, something else stayed. Something dense and silent.

Aryan sat among the noise but wasn't really in it. His elbow rested against the desk, head tilted, trying to look like he cared. The professor's words floated somewhere behind his thoughts, not quite a lecture, more like background weather.

He rubbed his temple, trying to look awake. But his mind was hooked elsewhere.

On her.

Sara. Not at the center of the room, but near the window. Half in light, half in her own world. She didn't try to disappear, but she also didn't ask to be noticed. Her fingers rested over the window sill, calm, composed.

She wasn't taking notes. She wasn't performing attention. She was just there. And somehow, that felt like a statement.

He watched her the way people stare at something they can't name. This wasn't the girl who traded quickfire comebacks or who laughed like she was sculpting air. This version of Sara was more reserved, different. Not smaller, just... harder to decode.

Her silence wasn't void. It had edges, a kind of spine. It didn't hide her; it defined her.

He leaned slightly forward, as if his body was trying to listen better than his ears.

"Drifting off, or planning an escape?" he asked. It came out softer than he meant, more curiosity than joke.

Sara didn't react. She turned, slow and sure, and for a few seconds, something real passed between them. Not history. Just recognition.

"Bit of both," she said, her voice low and clear. "Can't decide whether I want to vanish… or be found."

Her eyes stayed on him a beat too long before she looked away. A small smile followed, one that didn't ask to be noticed.

Some smiles aren't responses.
They're decisions.

Something inside Aryan tightened. Not like attraction, but like awareness. Like he'd just stumbled into someone in the middle of changing.

"You planning to leave the rest of us behind?" he asked, half serious.

She met his gaze, unbothered. "Only the ones not paying attention."

The corner of his mouth twitched. He looked down, pretending to adjust his pen. She chewed her pen cap without realizing. For a moment, they were both faking focus. Two people caught between pretending and presence.

The day peeled forward.

ENTERING IT

There comes a point when silence stops being space and starts becoming invitation. It isn't about crossing a line. It's about standing close enough to feel something change in the air.

The library that day wasn't special. Same tables, same low buzz, same half-focused students pretending to read. But something in the way they both stayed began to mean more than either could admit.

Between them, words became almost secondary. It wasn't about talking anymore. It was about being there, long enough for understanding to settle into its own kind of gravity.

They weren't defining anything, not naming or forcing it. Just learning to listen differently. To the space between questions. To the comfort in not rushing. And maybe, to the simple fact that she hadn't left when everyone else did.

They found each other again later, differently. The library this time. A bunker of fading voices and unreal deadlines. Their group had collapsed around a table, the usual scene: scattered papers, half-hearted focus, caffeine sweat.

Aryan spoke just enough to seem involved, but his mind wandered again. Sara sat across, scribbling notes, correcting others, catching flaws before they grew. She was sharp. Clear. Efficient.

But behind it, he noticed the small things.

Her fingers tapping the pen in an uneven beat. Her jaw tightening every few minutes. Small signs of unease that didn't match her calm surface.

"You always tap like that when you're thinking?" he asked, voice low.

She looked up, eyebrow raised. "I tap when I want to stay grounded. Better than disappearing mid-sentence."

He nodded. "You ever feel like you're holding back a flood?"

"Sometimes," she said after a pause. "But floods don't help in places built on silence."

It wasn't what she said that hit him. It was what she didn't. The space her words left behind felt heavier than the ones she used.

He almost said something else, almost filled the air. But she'd already turned back to her notes. Her shoulders squared. Her attention reassembled itself.

She was good at that. Building walls that didn't look like walls.

The others moved off out one by one. The library exhaled. Power stayed low. Books settled back into themselves.

Sara stayed.

Her notebook was open, but she wasn't writing. Her hands rested on the edges of the page, unmoving, waiting for something she couldn't quite name.

Aryan stood nearby for a while before walking over.

"You're still here," he said.

"I could say the same about you."

He leaned against the table, arms folded. "You stuck?"

"Not on the project," she said, closing the notebook harder than needed. "Just… in general."

No drama. Just truth, plain and spoken.

He didn't pry. Just nodded, staying there, a witness instead of a fixer.

"You're a labyrinth, Sara," he said finally.

She blinked. "That sounds poetic. And mildly insulting."

"I mean it," he said. "You don't show people where the doors are. But that doesn't mean they're not there."

Her mouth twitched. "Maybe I don't want them to find the way in."

"Maybe the ones who try don't want to get out."

Some connections aren't built for entry or exit. They're meant to be dwelled in.

She stood, slow and firm, the chair barely scraping. "You always talk like that?"

"Only when I'm not trying to impress anyone."

A soft breath passed between them. Not awkward. Just real.

She slung her bag over one shoulder. "See you tomorrow?"

He nodded.

But he didn't leave right away. Not even after she did. The air still held her shape somehow. Something unsaid, but not gone. Something structured enough to stay.

SHE, UNCHARTED

Some people can't be figured out, and maybe they're not supposed to be. They aren't puzzles waiting for someone smart enough to solve them, not exactly. They're just… whole on their own terms. Sara was like that. She didn't hide, she just didn't fit into neat explanations.

Aryan stopped trying to read her like a map. He just wanted to be near enough to see what moved under the surface. Being around her wasn't about getting answers. It was about learning to sit with the parts that don't explain themselves.

Not everything needs to be understood. Some people just need to be seen from the edge, not examined, not labeled. Just witnessed, gently, without taking anything from them.

CHAPTER 04

Gates Without Locks

Conversations are the bridges we build to cross the unknown, one word at a time.

After the elective class, Aryan went back to his room, dropped his bag on the chair, then sat on the edge of his bed like he wasn't sure whether to lie down or get up again.

He wasn't tired.
He was… wired.
Buzzing in a low-key way, like his thoughts were moving but refusing to talk to him.

Sara had left the room hours ago, but somehow she hadn't. She was still sitting in the air. Still in his head. Still in the uncomfortable space behind his ribs.

Not crush.
Not infatuation.
Just… something.

He checked his phone without meaning to. Screen on. Nothing new. Screen off. Back on again. He rubbed his thumb across his lip, then caught himself and exhaled like he was annoyed at his own brain.

He opened their group chat.

Everyone else talked like words were cheap.
Sara typed like each one cost something.

He hovered over the keyboard for way too long, thumb tapping the screen, then stopping, then tapping again like he was trying to trick the phone into choosing for him.

Then he typed.

Aryan: That thing you said in class today about companies needing to feel consequences locally? Bold move. Especially with the prof worshipping global scale like it's a religion.

He hit send before he could overthink it.
Instant regret. He almost threw the phone aside just to escape his own message.

Read.
Typing dots.
Then,

Sara: Someone had to interrupt the TED-talk energy. Glad at least one person was awake.

He gave a short laugh, paused, then shook his head. Okay. She was sharp. And she didn't soften edges for anyone.

Aryan: You rearranged the room without raising your voice. That's a talent.

Sara: Grew up with siblings. Silence is only useful if it's loaded.

He leaned back against the wall.
Yeah. That tracked.

They kept going. Class jokes, professor jokes, harmless stuff. But under the surface, something moved. Like there was a door open somewhere neither of them wanted to acknowledge yet.

Aryan: If you could leave and go anywhere right now, where?

A pause. No typing dots. He almost regretted asking.

Then she answered.

Sara: Bhutan.

Straight. No hesitation.

He could picture her saying it in person: calm, sure, not trying to impress anyone.

Aryan: Not even thinking twice.

Sara: Why would I? The mountains, the calm… it feels like another world. No need to perform happiness because they measure real joy. I think I'd breathe differently there.

He smiled. Not a dramatic smile, just a small one that surprised him when he felt it.

Aryan: I'd chart all the trails for you.

Sara: Assuming I'd want company? Bold.

He laughed low in his throat. Ran his hand through his hair, suddenly aware he was smiling at a screen like an idiot.

Aryan: Okay fine, I'd leave clues. You could decide whether to follow or ditch me.

Sara: That sounds like you. Complicate the simple path.

Something eased between them. Playful, but real.

Then she changed her tone.

Sara: Do you ever feel like there's another version of you? Not the one people see. The one that actually exists?

He froze halfway through typing a joke. Deleted the half sentence.

He cracked his knuckles.
God. Why did nerves show up now?

Aryan: Yeah. All the time. The real one's messier. I hide him well.

A few seconds.
Then she replied

Sara: Same. Hiding feels easier than being misread.

Aryan: Maybe conversations like this help. Slow exit from the mask.

She didn't reply right away. He watched the typing bubble appear, vanish, return.

Sara: Maybe the point isn't taking the mask off all at once. Maybe it's letting someone see the cracks first.

He exhaled softly.
Not the dramatic love-story sigh, just the kind where your chest feels too full and you need to let some air go.

Words slowed, but nothing felt unfinished. They slid into small truths. Losing people. Ambitions that felt heavier than inspiring. The fear of being misunderstood. Nothing dramatic, just the soft parts no one says out loud on purpose.

When the chat finally ended, it didn't feel like an ending.

It felt like a gate standing open. Not wide. Just enough to know someone hadn't shut it.

Aryan placed his phone face-down.
Stared at the ceiling.
Let a small, involuntary smile escape.

Somewhere across campus, Sara probably did the same.

No big truths. No promises. No drama.

Just the first real connection.

A beginning with no name yet,
and no lock.

Just an open gate.

It wasn't love.
It wasn't certainty.
Just two people letting someone see a softer angle
of them. Slow. Cautious. Brave in tiny ways.

Sometimes that's where everything actually starts.

CHAPTER 05

The Grammar of Nearness

Time spent with someone is the clearest expression of what they mean to you.

There wasn't a moment where things "clicked." It didn't happen with a reveal or a sharp turn. It was slower than that. Day by day, they just stopped trying so hard, stopped proving, stopped second-guessing, stopped guarding every feeling like it was a secret that needed armor. What used to feel tense or uncertain became… familiar. Not perfect, not dramatic. Just real.

They weren't analysing every silence anymore. They weren't wondering what every look meant. They were just showing up, in hallways, in messages, in those tiny pockets of the day where most people pass each other without noticing. Time together stopped feeling accidental. It became a habit. A soft one. The kind that sneaks up on you.

Nothing big changed on the face of things. No label. No big promise. Just presence. The kind that doesn't need to be announced because it keeps happening anyway. And in that repetition, something found its place. Not a conclusion, not even a certainty… but a comfort. A slow-growing trust. The kind that doesn't need a show to feel real.

Sometimes you don't realize someone matters until they're simply there, again and again, and life feels slightly heavier in their absence. That's where Aryan and Sara found themselves. Not rushing toward anything. Just staying. And somehow, staying was enough.

Time didn't arrive with a bang for them. It wasn't dramatic or cinematic. It just… stayed. Day by day, little by little. Aryan didn't chase feelings anymore; he watched how people used their minutes. Who they gave their time to. Who they showed up for when nothing big was happening.

With Sara, time didn't feel spent, it felt collected. Like it was piling up somewhere, gently forming something neither of them was naming yet.

Their messages weren't deep, but they kept happening. Their goodbyes lasted a little longer than necessary. When she walked toward him, his shoulders softened without him realizing. When he saw her car pull in, something in his chest settled, like it already knew where to go.

That Friday, the text came short and casual:

Sara: "Need to grab a book from the library. You around?"
Aryan: "Yeah. I'll come."
Sara: "Okay. Ten minutes."

He didn't rush. Didn't fix his hair in the mirror like a desperate teenager. But he did check it once. Just once. And he walked out a little faster than usual.

Her car rolled in. Her cousin was driving. Aryan stuffed his hands in his pockets and pretended he wasn't suddenly overly aware of his walk. She stepped out, wearing a white shirt, jeans, hair tied up but already loosening. Not trying to impress anybody, but somehow impossible not to look at.

She waved to her cousin. A small smile. That tiny family moment made Aryan realize he knew nothing about her world outside these moments. The thought surprised him, and yeah, it stung a little, but in a curious way, not a hurt way.

She spotted him and smirked.
"You're early."

He shrugged, trying to look casual. "Traffic gods were kind." It sounded stupid. Whatever. She smiled anyway.

Inside the library, she scanned shelves like she was looking for a part of herself she misplaced. He stayed close but didn't hover. Just... there.

She finally spoke, still reading book spines.
"Behavioral psychology. For class. And because I'm trying to figure out why some people crumble while others don't."

He leaned a little closer. "And you?"
A moment. A breath.
"That's for you to find out."

He didn't push. He just nodded, jaw tightening for a second, holding nerves he'd never admit.

Later, on the terrace, the sun was doing that warm, late-evening thing that makes even doubts soften. Sara leaned on the railing, tapping her fingers like her thoughts were pacing.

"Relationships exhaust me," she said, without looking over. "Everyone wants everything."

Aryan looked up from his book, thumb holding the page. "Maybe the right ones don't drain you. They refill you."

"That sounds cute," she said, half-scoff, half-truth she wasn't ready to unpack.

He grinned. "Cute's underrated."

She stared at him a little too long.
"Don't get poetic on me."

"Wouldn't dare."
He wasn't poetic. But he meant every damn word.

Something settled differently there. Nothing big. Just a tiny click in the background of the moment. Like both of them felt something found its place, but neither of them named it.

After that day, they didn't get bigger, they just kept showing up.

She found herself noticing him without meaning to.
The way he tilted his head before asking something real.
The way he didn't fill silence. Just sat in it with her, hands loose, presence relaxed.
He didn't try to fix her pauses. He didn't chase her walls.

And that terrified her more than any intense romance ever had.
Because he wasn't trying to get in.
He just wasn't leaving.

One evening in the courtyard, she exhaled like she'd been holding something too long.
"I'm not good at letting people close. I'm scared they'll see the parts I don't like."

Aryan leaned back, fingers laced behind his head. He didn't rush. Didn't soften his voice to sound wise. Just spoke like someone who actually lived his words.

"Everyone has unfinished parts. Doesn't make you harder to love."

She didn't respond. But her foot stopped tapping. Her shoulders dropped a little. She stayed. That was answer enough.

By the end of the week, she caught herself thinking about him in the middle of random conversations. In the car. Brushing her teeth. Mid-sentence once, and her cousin noticed.

"You're different lately," he teased. "Who's the guy?"

Sara looked away. "Nobody."
Then softer, like she was correcting herself:
"Just someone who's around."

Later that night, she opened her phone. No new message.

But for the first time, she didn't panic at the silence.
It felt warm. Unrushed.
Like something growing roots instead of wings.

She smiled. Small. Almost secret.

Hope didn't knock this time.
It just sat beside her, like it belonged, waiting.

And she didn't tell it to leave.

CHAPTER 06

The Roots We Carry

To know someone, you eventually meet their world: their people, their spaces, the unguarded parts they don't explain.

The change didn't happen all at once. It was slow, the kind you only notice once you're already living it.

She wasn't just someone he texted at odd hours anymore. She was in his days now. In the in-betweens. In the way he checked his phone without meaning to.

There were still parts of her he hadn't seen. Names she mentioned lightly. Stories she skipped. And one of those names had been Shiv.

Saturday.

Sara: Coffee?
Aryan: Always. Where?
Sara: Near my uncle's. Might bring my cousin.

That last line hit different.

Not nerves, more like something close. A doorway opening.

An hour later, Aryan stood outside the café. No fancy sign. Just a chalkboard menu and a door that squeaked every time someone pushed it open. He wiped his palms on his jeans; more habit than nerves.

Sara arrived with that calm energy she always carried, hair slightly messy like she'd tied it in the car. Shiv followed a step behind, slim, observant, the kind of person who sees before he speaks.

"This is him," Sara said simply. "Aryan — Shiv."

Shiv shook his hand, firm but not trying to prove anything.

"She keeps mentioning you," Shiv said.

Aryan laughed lightly. "Hope it's not as a warning."

Shiv smirked. "If it was, you wouldn't be here."

No drama. Just a fact.

They slid into a booth. The table wobbled Aryan tried to adjust it with a tissue under the leg, didn't work, let it go. Coffee shops don't test character, but sometimes small things do.

The playlist was some slow 2000s love song.

"This music is… bold," Shiv said.

Aryan shrugged. "Better than elevator music."

Shiv nodded like that was fair.

Their coffees arrived, and nobody touched them right away. Sara stirred sugar into hers and spilled a little on the table; wiped it with her sleeve. Real, casual, unbothered. He liked that.

"So," Shiv said, leaning back. "Has she told you about her Chicken Wings obsession?"

Sara groaned. "Shiv. Stop."

Aryan raised an eyebrow at her. "Wings? That's your secret?"

"She destroys them," Shiv continued, ignoring her. "I've seen her take down an embarrassing number of plates at food stalls. Like, legitimately scary."

Sara covered her face. "I hate you."

Aryan smiled. "Okay, wings next time. Noted."

Sara flicked a sugar packet at Shiv. He didn't even block; just laughed.

Humor is an entry pass. Not a test. You laugh your way in, or you don't get in at all.

Sara got a call and stepped outside. Her phone lit up with "Uncle."
Aryan pretended not to notice. Shiv didn't pretend.

Suddenly it was just the two of them.
No soft landing. Just silence and coffee steam.

Shiv took a slow sip. "So."

Aryan matched him. "So."

"What's the deal with you two?"

Aryan didn't overthink. "It fits. Doesn't need fixing."

Shiv sat with that for a second. Then nodded. "She doesn't let people in easily. But you're here, so you must've done something right."

It wasn't approval. It was recognition.

Belonging isn't announced. It shows up in one unforced sentence.

"Don't drop the thread," Shiv added, voice low but unburdened. "She's special. Not everyone gets invited in."

Before Aryan could reply, Sara walked back in. "What are you two talking about?"

Shiv: "Weather."

Sara squinted at both of them. Let it drop.

"Uncle's waiting."

The drive to her uncle's house was full of casual teasing and half arguments about music. Shiv played something loud and cheesy. Sara hit skip. He cursed. Aryan just laughed in the backseat, feeling something warm he hadn't realized he missed, being around people who had history with each other.

Her uncle's house was simple, lived-in. Shoes by the door, a faint smell of incense and fried onions. Uncle shook Aryan's hand, sure and warm.

"So. You're the one I've heard about," he said.

No smile. No frown. Just presence.

Aryan smiled. "I hope she exaggerated the good parts."

Uncle chuckled. "She doesn't exaggerate anything."

They talked. Books. Careers. Random little things. No heavy questions. No spotlight. Just warmth spread thin and even.

At one point, Uncle leaned back. "People you meet at this age, they matter more than you realize."

Aryan glanced at Sara. She didn't look back, but her shoulder relaxed. That was enough.

By the time they were leaving, Shiv tapped Aryan's shoulder. "You're alright. Better than I expected."

"Wow," Aryan replied. "High praise."

Shiv shrugged. "Smart men don't trip over expectations."

Sara rolled her eyes but smiled.

Sara walked with Aryan to the gate. Outside the gate, evening settling in:

"You can take a cab from here," she said.

"I've got someone coming."

A brief moment. No rush. Street dogs barking in the background. Some kid riding past on a cycle yelling at his friend.

"Thanks for coming," she said.

"Thanks for asking."

"Monday?"

He didn't make a big moment of it. "Always."

Not dramatic.
Not poetic.
Just true.

And this time, it felt like he wasn't just visiting her life.

He'd stepped inside it.

Connections take time.
Sometimes it's as simple as showing up, sitting in a
room that isn't yours yet, and letting the silence do
the work.

Belonging isn't gifted. It grows.
Not in big moves, but in the small ones where
nobody performs, and everyone is simply real.

CHAPTER 07

What I Had to Say

Staying silent
hurts more than saying the wrong thing.

The campus breeze had that post-evening-class chill: damp grass, dust kicked up from the football ground, a faint smell of samosas someone was still frying near the canteen.

Aryan kept shifting the strap of his backpack from one shoulder to the other.
Left. Right. Back again. He didn't even notice he was doing it.

They had spent an hour lying on the lawn, talking about everything and nothing, professors, inside jokes, childhood stories, her cousin's fridge magnet addiction (he'd laughed too loud at that one, like a stupid hiccup laugh that wouldn't stop). He had even thrown a tiny pebble at her and missed by a foot. She had rolled her eyes in that I-pretend-I-don't-find-you-funny way.

Now they were walking.

No inside jokes.
Just footsteps and the occasional leaf crunching.

Sara was scrolling her phone with one thumb, screen lighting her face every few seconds, not really typing anything. Aryan kept glancing at his own screen too, not opening the notifications. Pretend-busy hands are better than empty hands.

Somewhere in between, Shiv's name had come up. Just in passing. Not dramatic. But he had felt it, that small change in her tone. Warmth reserved. The way someone talks about a person who exists in a slightly softer corner of their brain.

He hadn't said anything then. Just laughed at some dumb follow-up story she told. But that name had settled in his chest like a pebble stuck in a shoe.

They walked slower without noticing.

Aryan swallowed. A quick one. Then another, trying to hide it. Like his throat wanted to bail out of the moment before the rest of him did.

Say it now.

He opened his mouth, closed it, scratched his neck for no reason. His backpack strap slipped off again; he caught it like it mattered.

"Sara."

She looked up immediately, not surprised. More like she had already sensed the air getting heavy. She tucked a loose hair behind her ear and bit her lower lip once, quick, as if bracing.

"Yeah?"

Aryan slowed his steps. "There's something I—" He exhaled, shaking his head at himself. "I've been meaning to tell you something."

Sara stopped walking. Just like that. As if she knew. Her expression shifted, curiosity, then something softer, unreadable. "You're being serious all of a sudden."

"I don't know when it happened," Aryan started, words slow, careful like stepping on broken glass, "but somewhere between your everyday stories and… you just existing the way you do, I ended up… liking you. More than I meant to."

Her fingers tightened around the strap of her bag. Just a little. Just enough to notice.

He tried again, voice clearer now:

"You're the first person I think about in the morning."
He paused.
"And the last one before I sleep."

Silence. Not heavy. Just real. Someone cycled past, tyre making that soft gravel crunch.

Sara's throat moved. She swallowed too. A mix of empathy and discomfort.

"Aryan…" she started, choosing each word like it might detonate. "There's someone I've been… talking to. And I think he's becoming important to me."

His jaw tightened for half a second. Then eased. He nodded once, then again, the second nod slower, more honest.

"Okay."
A beat.
"Okay."

The first one was instinct. The second was acceptance dragging itself out.

"I just didn't want to pretend I didn't hear this inside me anymore," he said quietly. "I wasn't trying to… win anything. I just needed you to know."

"I respect that," she said. Her voice wasn't pity. It was careful, but warm. "And I don't want to lose what we have. I really don't."

"You won't," he said. "I don't think feelings disappear just because they don't... evolve. They just... settle. Different place. Still real."

He shrugged, but his hands stayed clenched inside his pockets, knuckles tight with tension.

She smiled, small, tired, grateful. No performance in it. "I'm glad you told me."

He exhaled, something between release and weight. "Me too."

They stood there another moment. Wind rustled fallen leaves around their shoes. He kicked one, barely, just to do something with his foot.

"I should go," she said, backing toward the parking area.

"Yeah," he nodded. "Drive safe."

She looked at him once more, not asking to stay, not pulling away either, then walked to her car and started the engine. Headlights washed over him for a second before she pulled off and disappeared down the road.

He didn't move until the tail lights vanished.

No collapsing.
No background noise.

Just a boy who finally said the thing that had been
chewing through him.

He shoved his hands deeper into his pockets and started
walking.
Campus felt the same, but he didn't.
The night wasn't darker. It was just honest now.

Sometimes you speak not to change someone's heart.
Just to stop lying to your own.

CHAPTER 08

The Spaces Between

What isn't said still speaks.

The silence between them had started to feel normal. Comfortable, even.

But Aryan couldn't shake the weight of their last talk. It hovered around him, not sharp or painful, just unfinished, like a sentence someone forgot to end.

Sara had mentioned someone else. Not like it mattered. Just slipped it in, like tossing a pebble into a pond and walking away before the ripples showed.
It should've cleared things up. But it didn't. Something heavier stayed behind.

Days passed. The group project kept them circling the same space.
They'd sit near each other, trade notes, talk logistics, and that was enough.
Still, Aryan noticed small changes. The way Sara's guard sometimes dropped for half a second before coming back. The way her laugh, rare as it was, still reached him.

He didn't chase it. He just let it happen.

Late afternoon. Library.
The building was half-empty, the spin of ceiling fans the only sound. Dust floated in slanted light.
Sara sat at the far end of the table, pen twirling between her fingers.
Her phone lay face down beside a half-open notebook.

Aryan walked in, his bag slung over one shoulder. He pulled out the chair across from her, dragging it a little louder than needed.

"You'd think group projects would actually involve a group," she said, not looking up. But her mouth curved, barely.

"Maybe they trust us to carry them," he said.

"Or maybe they just know we will," she replied, tapping her pen once against the table.

They worked silently.
Pages turned. Screens glowed. The air carried a soft pulse, typing, a cough in the distance, a chair squeaking somewhere.

After a while, Aryan leaned back, stretching. His chair creaked.
"So," he said, "any chance I can distract you for a bit?"

Sara looked up, eyebrow raised. "What kind of distraction?"

"The good kind," he said.

She smiled, faintly. Then, leaning back too, said, "Go on. Distract me."

He hadn't planned that far. For a moment, he just looked at her. The way her hair fell forward when she tilted her head. The soft click of her pen. The light catching the edge of her wristwatch.
And then it slipped out:

"What memory keeps you anchored?"

Sara paused. Her eyes dropped to the table.
"That's not a small one," she said, like the words had weight. Then, after a beat:
"Maybe… weekends with my uncle. Drives with my cousin and the dogs. Cooking something simple. Watching dumb movies. No noise, no pressure. Just being."

She said it plain. No attempt to sound deep. But the silence after carried weight.
Her fingers brushed the corner of her notebook, tracing the edge. "It's strange what stays," she said softly.

Aryan watched her, the small movements. The way her voice rose just enough, then retreated.
"Maybe they stay because they're still teaching us," he said.

Sara looked up, half-smiling. "You sound like a self-help book. Is that your thing?"

He shrugged. "Only on Tuesdays."

She shook her head, amused. But she didn't look away this time. Something in the air eased. No clarity. No confession. Just calm.

After a moment, he said, "I used to think peace meant being alone. Reading. Shutting everything out. But now I think it's being next to someone and not needing to talk. Just being there."

Sara nodded, slowly. "Yeah. That's… real." Her voice had softened. "It's balance, I guess."

They didn't push the moment. They let it rest, silent and enough.

Then came the noise, the rest of their teammates: loud, laughing, late. The air changed.

Sara turned toward them, slipping back into the group like habit. Her laughter mixed with theirs easily.

Aryan stayed seated, closing his notebook but not getting up. He watched her from a distance, not with longing, not regret. Just watching.

The sun had dropped by the time they packed up. The last light hit the floor in thin orange lines.
Sara left with the others. She didn't look back.

He could've followed.
He didn't.

Something between them had taken root, not spoken aloud, not named, but real.

CHAPTER 09

The Other Side of the Mirror

Sometimes another person sees the version of you you didn't know existed.

The morning was ordinary. Nothing unusual. People moved around Aryan the way they always did, students rushing, someone arguing on the phone, someone yawning into a coffee cup. But he moved slower. Something in him felt tilted, like a chair leg placed on uneven floor.

He kept replaying the conversation with Sara, but it wasn't the words. It was how she didn't rush the unspoken spaces. She didn't try to fill them or rescue him from them. She just… let them sit. And somehow, that stayed with him more than anything she said.

His phone buzzed.

Sara: Art exhibition at 5. Come with me?

He stared at the message. His first reaction was no. Art wasn't his thing. It made him feel stupid. People stared at paintings and pretended to understand them. He preferred things that came with structure, steps, reasons.

But he typed anyway.

Aryan: Sure. Why not.

He didn't know why he said yes. Maybe curiosity. Maybe her.

The gallery was small. The kind of place you walked past without noticing. Inside, it smelled faintly of dust and old air-conditioning.

Sara waved when she saw him. She wasn't dressed up; she didn't act like she needed to be. She just stood comfortably in her own space; hands tucked into her jacket pockets.

"You made it," she said.

He nodded. "Still time to escape."

"Not allowed," she said, already smiling.

They walked in. A few people wandered around, speaking softly as if the paintings would get offended.

Sara stopped at one large piece. "Okay. Tell me what you see."

Aryan squinted at it. "Honestly? Looks like someone got angry and took it out on their canvas."

She snorted. "Wow. Incredible depth. Truly enlightening."

"It's your fault for asking."

She shook her head and stepped a little closer to the painting. "Just try. Don't analyze it. Look at it and see what comes up."

He tried. For about two seconds. Then he glanced at her instead. She leaned in just enough to study the corner of the canvas, as if it mattered. Her mouth relaxed. Her shoulders dropped. She looked… peaceful.

"I don't get it," he said softly.

"Get what?"

"You. This. How this does something for you."

She thought for a second, eyes still on the painting. "It lets me breathe," she said. "I don't have to be anything here."

He nodded but didn't answer.

They kept moving. Every now and then she'd ask him what he thought. He'd give some ridiculous answer; she'd roll her eyes; he'd pretend to be offended; she'd laugh. It felt simple. Easy. Nothing heavy.

They stopped in front of a sculpture, twisted metal, slightly rusted.

"What about this?" she asked.

"Looks like leftover construction pieces," he said.

She laughed, too loud for the room. A few people turned. She didn't care.

"Okay, try again," she said.

He slipped his hands into his pockets. "I think… it looks like something that was meant to be one thing but ended up becoming something else."

She blinked. He didn't know if she was surprised or just thinking.

"That's actually good," she said softly.

They moved on. At some point, their hands brushed. Neither of them commented. Neither pulled away. His chest tightened. Not big. Just a slight move, like someone adjusting the volume on a radio.

When they stepped outside, the air was colder than he expected. Sara rubbed her palms together and blew into them.

"Thanks for coming," she said. "I know this is not your world."

"It wasn't terrible," he said. "Though I'm still convinced half of those artists just threw random stuff around and called it a day."

She bumped her shoulder into his. "You don't know anything."

"And yet here I am, still surviving."

She laughed again. It was the kind of laugh that wasn't hiding anything.

They reached her car. She stopped, keys in hand.

"Well," she said.

"Yeah."

A small pause. Not awkward. Just there.

"Good night, Aryan."

"Good night."

She got in. He stepped back and watched her reverse out of the parking space. The red tail lights pulled away and disappeared down the road.

He stood there longer than necessary, hands in pockets, breath visible in the cold air.

He remembered what she'd said inside: just feel.

Maybe he still didn't understand art. Maybe he wouldn't ever.

But tonight wasn't about the art.

It was about her.

And the strange, gentle realization that someone had held up a mirror, and for a second, he saw a version of himself he didn't hate.

He didn't know what this meant.
He only knew he felt different walking out than he did
walking in.

CHAPTER 10

The Middle of Things

Most changes are slow until suddenly they're not.

The night wasn't epic. The road wasn't glowing. Nothing special was happening.

Aryan and Sara just walked side by side, hands in pockets, matching each other's pace without trying to. Every few seconds, Aryan kicked a loose stone ahead. Sara kept adjusting the strap of her bag like it was too long.

It felt silent in a way that wasn't uncomfortable.

Out of nowhere, Sara said, "You've been holding your breath all evening."

Aryan let out a short exhale, half-laugh, half-release. "Maybe I didn't realise."

She looked at him straight on, not dramatic, just honest. "That's not nothing."

He rubbed the back of his neck, eyes flicking toward a parked bike like it might help. "Do you ever feel like you're carrying a version of yourself that doesn't even feel like you anymore?"

She frowned a little. "What does that mean?"

He stopped walking for a second. "Like you ended up becoming someone out of… circumstances. People. Expectations. Things you didn't even agree to, but now you're stuck performing them."

Sara slowed too, shifting her weight to one leg. "That's a lot."

He shrugged. "Yeah."

They kept walking.

After a bit, they reached a patch of uneven pavement under a large tree. Sara nudged a fallen twig with her shoe. Aryan sat down on the low boundary wall nearby, elbows on knees. She stayed standing for a moment before sitting beside him, leaving enough space so neither felt boxed in.

"I used to be more… unfiltered," Aryan said, eyes on his hands. "I'd say what I felt, even if it didn't sound perfect. I don't know when I stopped doing that."

Sara didn't say anything. She just pulled her hair behind one ear and waited.

"It's not some tragic thing," he added quickly. "It's just… people expect things. Or you think they do. And then you start trimming your rough edges because you don't want to disappoint anyone."

She nodded once. Small, simple, no analysis.

Aryan let out a slow breath. "It's weird missing a version of yourself you don't know how to return to."

He glanced at her. "What about you? What's under your silence?"

Sara's fingers curled around the edge of the wall. A tiny movement, but it said enough.

"There are things I'm not ready to talk about," she said. "Not because they're heavy. Just… not ready."

He didn't push. He just nodded and looked back at the street. Someone pedalled past on a cycle, the chain clicking loudly. The moment grounded itself again.

For a while, they didn't talk. Sara pulled a loose thread from her sleeve. Aryan tapped his foot against the wall. Their silences didn't clash.

Eventually, without deciding, both stood up. Aryan brushed dust off his jeans. Sara tightened her bag strap again.

As they walked, slower now, Aryan asked, "Do you think it's possible to move ahead without dragging everything from before?"

She was silent for a few seconds. Then she said, "I think we carry it no matter what. But maybe it doesn't have to feel like a punishment. Maybe it's something you build with."

He nodded, not fully convinced, but not rejecting it either.

"Hard to believe," he said.

"Most real things are," she answered simply.

The road split ahead. The streetlights weren't bright enough, so their shadows stretched weirdly across the concrete.

They stopped at the junction.

Aryan shoved his hands back into his pockets. "Thanks for walking with me."

Sara's voice softened. "Thanks for sharing."

He didn't expect that to hit as hard as it did.

She took two steps away, then turned back for a second.

"For what it's worth," she said, "you're not behind. You're just… in the middle of things."

Then she walked off. No special exit. No long look. Just a straightforward departure that somehow felt gentle.

Aryan stood there for a moment, adjusting his sleeves, breathing slower than before. Something small inside him changed, not fixed, not solved, just changed.

Maybe that was enough for the night.

CHAPTER 11

Something's Off

Sometimes things change silently,
and no one knows how to bring it up first.

Campus mornings still sounded the same, chairs dragging, the canteen mixer whirring, some senior yelling someone's nickname across the corridor. But between Aryan and Sara, something small had changed. Not a fight. Not a misunderstanding. Just… a loosened knot.

She wasn't avoiding him.
He wasn't angry.
But neither of them felt like they were in the same room at the same time anymore.

It showed up in tiny ways, the missed eye contact, the shorter replies, the way both of them paused half a second before speaking, as if measuring the distance first.

Nobody else would've noticed.

They felt it instantly.

In their elective class, Aryan caught Sara looking in his direction.
Not at him.
Past him.
Like her eyes were searching for something behind his face.

She was scribbling in her notebook, faster than usual, the tip of her pen scratching a little too hard. They used to joke about how round her handwriting looked. Today it looked like it had edges.

He thought of leaning over and asking what she was writing.
But she didn't seem available for interruptions.

He shifted in his seat and stared at the board, pretending he was listening. He wasn't.

Later, in the canteen, they bumped into each other, literally by accident.
Sara was turning with a tray; he was reaching for a bottle of water on the counter.

Their hands brushed the same bottle.
She pulled back too quickly.

"Oh, sorry," she said.

"No, it's fine," Aryan replied.

Both gave a half-smile; the kind people use to mask awkwardness. Then she took a seat two tables away instead of joining him like she normally would.

He pretended not to notice.

That evening, Sara sat on her bed with her knees up, phone resting on them. She was scrolling without reading anything. Ananya's name flashed on the screen.

She picked up on the fourth ring.

"Hey."

"You look exhausted," Ananya said, squinting at her through the camera. "What happened? Did someone steal your lunch?"

Sara let out a small laugh. "Nothing like that. Just… been a long week."

"Long week meaning college? Or long week meaning someone?"

Sara exhaled. "Maybe. Just… classes… and stuff."

"'Stuff' is the vocabulary of people who are avoiding the actual thing," Ananya said. "So, out with it."

Sara hesitated, rubbing the back of her neck. "It's just… someone I talk to a lot feels a bit distant lately. Maybe I'm imagining it."

Ananya smirked. "Uh-huh. 'Someone.' Let me guess, the same guy? The one you told me about?"

Sara rolled her eyes, but she didn't deny it. "He's just a friend."

"Sure," Ananya said. "And I'm Elon Musk."

Sara sighed. "It's not about labels. It's just, something feels off. He's silent more often. Slower to reply. Or maybe I'm reading too much into it."

Ananya shrugged. "Did something happen?"

"No."
Sara thought about the water bottle moment. The almost-smile. The looking away in class. "It's nothing big. Just… weird."

"Are you waiting for him to fix it?"

"No," she said quickly. Then slower: "Maybe. I don't know."

Ananya softened a little. "Look… maybe he's confused too. Or overwhelmed. Or scared he'll mess up whatever this is. Talking helps, you know."

Sara stared at the screen, not quite convinced.
"What if he doesn't feel it at all?"

"What if he does?" Ananya shot back.

Sara didn't answer.

Aryan was wandering around campus again. He didn't have a destination, just the need to move. He walked past the south canteen, past the dusty volleyball court, past the notice board where nobody ever read anything.

He ended up behind the library on the concrete steps, where the wind always carried someone else's conversation.

He sat and picked at a loose thread on his jeans.

He opened his chat with Sara.
The last thing there was a meme she'd sent.
He'd replied with a single laughing emoji.
It looked stupid now.

He whispered, "Why am I waiting for her to miss me?"

He didn't know if he wanted an answer or if he was scared of getting one.

So, he just sat there, letting the evening settle around him.

The next day, they walked out of class together. By habit, not intention.

Their steps synced automatically, like routine hadn't caught up to whatever was happening.

The corridor felt louder than usual. Their silence made it worse.

Sara cleared her throat. "Hey."

"Hey," he said.

That was it.

They walked a few more steps. He glanced at her. She kept her eyes forward.

She slowed. "I have to return a book to the library."

"Oh. Okay."

She nodded once. "See you around?"

"Yeah," he said. Too softly.

She walked away.

Aryan stayed where he was, replaying the conversation, which barely existed, trying to figure out if he'd missed a moment where he was supposed to say something honest.

Later that evening, Sara called Ananya again, lying on her side, facing the wall.

"He didn't ask anything," she said. "Didn't even pretend to."

Ananya frowned. "Is that what you wanted? For him to push?"

"I wanted him to… I don't know… notice." Her voice cracked a little on the last word.

"Maybe he did," Ananya said. "Maybe he's dealing with it in his own weird, silent way."

Sara pressed her thumb against the edge of her pillow. "Maybe I should've said something."

"Depends," Ananya said. "Do you want clarity? Or do you want to avoid saying something you can't take back?"

Sara exhaled, long and tired. "I want it to stop feeling like I'm guessing."

Ananya nodded. "Then you'll have to decide whether to ask or wait. Both are uncomfortable. But choose one."

"Or," Sara said low, "maybe the real ones don't rush. Maybe they step back before they ruin something."

Ananya didn't say anything to that.

Sara didn't end the call.
She just stayed there, listening to her friend breathe on the other end.

And for the first time all week,
she let herself admit it.
"I just wish I knew what changed."

CHAPTER 12

When We Finally Talked

Avoiding is easier. Talking is what saves things.

Some evenings don't end with clarity. They just stop. This was one of those.

The café was almost closing. Chairs scraped somewhere behind them. A staff guy wiped a table too loudly. The AC had given up. Outside, the rain was confused. Drizzling, stopping, picking up again. Everything felt half-done, including their conversation.

Aryan and Sara weren't fighting anymore, but they weren't fine either. They just sat there, facing each other, both tired from pretending they had nothing left to say.

The silence between them wasn't warm. But it wasn't cold either. It was just… real. Like both of them finally ran out of ways to avoid the main thing.

Aryan kept adjusting his cup even though it was already empty. Sara pulled her sleeves over her hands like she always did when she didn't know where to place her emotions.

He spoke first, mostly because he couldn't pretend anymore.

"Look… I messed up," he said low. "I panicked and shut down. I tried to not break anything, and that just made everything worse."

He wasn't saying it to earn forgiveness. He sounded like someone admitting something out loud for the first time.

Sara didn't jump in. Didn't soothe. Didn't offer a polite nod. She just listened, elbows on the table, hands clasped.

After a moment she said, "I didn't know if you were disappearing… or protecting yourself. And I didn't know how to ask without sounding desperate."

He looked at her then, really looked, and something in his face softened, not because he felt better, but because the truth finally landed between them.

"I didn't know closeness could be this confusing," he said. "I always assume I'll fail at it, so I pull back before anything can go wrong."

Sara leaned back in her chair. She didn't fold her arms, didn't guard herself. She looked tired, but present.

"I wasn't asking you to be perfect," she said. "I just needed to know where you were."

Her voice wasn't angry. It was honest in a way that didn't try to impress him.

"You're not impossible, Aryan. Just… hard to reach when you disappear into your own thoughts."

He exhaled. Not dramatically. Just like someone letting out air he was holding too long.

"I didn't think I deserved to be reached," he said.

That landed. Gently. No big reaction. Just a turn in the air.

Sara tapped her finger on the table a few times before speaking again.

"And maybe I didn't ask if you wanted to be understood," she said. "I assumed you did."

They both sat with that.
It wasn't a realization. It was just the truth. Finally said instead of assumed.

The café lights flickered once, meaning they should leave soon. Nobody moved.

"I want to try," Aryan said. "Not in some big way. Just… honestly. No running."

Sara nodded slowly. Not approval.
Just acknowledgment.

"Don't ask me to trust you yet," she said. "Just stay. We can see what happens from there."

He swallowed, nodded once.

"Okay," he said. "I can do that."

Outside, someone dropped a spoon on the floor. The sound broke the heaviness for a second.

Aryan rubbed his thumb over the handle of his mug. Sara pushed her hair behind her ear.

He asked, "What about you? Are you willing to face your part in this?"

She didn't answer immediately. She stared at a water ring on the table, circled it with her nail.

"I don't know," she said finally. "I want to. And if I do… I'd want you around."

That was probably the closest to vulnerability she'd given him in weeks.

He didn't grab her hand.
She didn't smile some movie-smile.

She just looked at him, firm, unsure, still choosing to stay.

"One step at a time?" she asked.

"One step at a time," he agreed.

There was no big hug. No music swelling. No sudden clarity.

Just two people sitting across from each other, finally saying the things they'd been avoiding. It wasn't a resolution. It wasn't a restart. It was a stop, a real one, where neither of them felt the need to pretend.

They stayed in their own chairs.
Their own corners.
Still separate, but not disconnected.

For now, that was enough.

Not everything needs to be solved to be real.
Some distances don't close in a moment.
Some conversations don't fix anything; they simply stop the silence from becoming permanent.

CHAPTER 13

The Night She Didn't Leave

Some people don't walk away.
They just step back until it feels safe again.

The city had gone silent in that strange way late evenings do. Traffic low, dogs barking somewhere far, someone shutting a balcony door. Nothing dramatic. Just the usual end-of-day sounds.

Sara sat on the edge of her bed, elbows on her knees, staring at the notepad on her lap. The page was still empty. She pressed the pen to it once, made a dot, and stopped. Pulled her hair back. Let it fall forward again. She'd walked around her room enough times to wear a path, from bed to window, from window to desk, back to bed. None of it helped. Her chest felt tight in that annoying, restless way where nothing is exactly wrong but nothing is fine either.

She kept telling herself she'd done the right thing earlier. That giving distance was responsible. That keeping her boundaries clear was healthier than letting him expect something she couldn't give.

But her stomach kept twisting anyway.

Across town, Aryan stood by his window, the light from his phone stretching across his wrist. He re-read their last message. He typed.

Aryan: Are you okay?

He paused, added another line.

Aryan: I know you said no calls, but… If it helps, I can be silent on the line. Just stay with me there.

He waited. The three dots appeared. Went away. Came back.

Sara: Okay. But only for a bit.

The call rang once. Twice. She picked up on the third.

Neither spoke.

It wasn't an intentional silence. It was just two people who didn't know where to start.

Sara shifted on her bed, pulling her knees up. Aryan sat down slowly, the chair creaking under him.

He spoke first. "You don't have to explain anything. Just... let's be here for a bit."

Sara rubbed her forehead. "I don't know what I'm doing, Aryan." Her voice came out thinner than she meant.

"I know," he said softly.

"It's not you," she muttered, the words breaking unevenly. "It's like... every time something feels real, I just... freeze. My whole body starts acting like it's a trap."

She let out a breath that wasn't quite a laugh. "I've seen things fall apart too many times. My parents' bond, friendships I thought were solid, relationships where I was half-present anyway... I don't trust myself to not mess things up."

Aryan didn't jump in. She heard him shift, maybe leaning back, maybe just listening harder.

"I told you I don't believe in walls," she said. "But I do. I build them fast. Then I act like it's clarity."

He smiled; she could hear it in his breath more than his tone. "I didn't believe you when you said that."

She blinked. "You didn't?"

"No. It sounded like you were trying to sound brave."

She swallowed. That landed somewhere uncomfortable but honest.

Another pause. She picked at a loose thread near her pillowcase.

"I don't want to be your almost," she said suddenly, her throat tightening as she spoke. "I don't want you waiting for me to grow up emotionally, or be better, or be less... whatever this is." She gestured around her room even though he couldn't see. "I don't want to be a project. Or someone you tolerate."

"You're not a maybe to me," he said, firm but not dramatic. "You're just you. And I'm here because of that."

She pushed her nail against the spine of the notebook. "You're grounded. I'm a mess. I'm scared I won't catch up."

"There's nothing to catch up to," he said gently. "It's not a race."

She exhaled, shaky. "I don't know how long I'll need."

"Then you need long," he replied. "That's okay."

She looked at her ceiling for a moment. "And if I shut down again? If I say something stupid trying to protect myself?"

"I'll breathe," he said. "And I'll ask again later. We don't have to fix everything the second it happens."

She pressed her forehead against her knee for a moment. The tightness in her chest didn't disappear, but it loosened a little, like someone had turned down the volume of the fear.

"I keep thinking," she admitted softly, "that if I say yes to anything with you, I'm going to lose parts of myself."

"Or maybe you'll find the ones you hid," he said, his voice low, almost an exhale.

She didn't answer. Not immediately. The silence wasn't heavy now, just slow.

Finally, she said, "That's what scares me the most."

"Then be scared," he replied. "Just don't run because of it. We can walk through it. Even if we look stupid doing it."

She let out a small, real laugh. The first of the night.

Her voice softened. "I want to try. But on my terms. At my pace."

"I'm with you," he said. "Even if it's slow."

They didn't hang up.

After a while, the conversation moved on. They talked about the assignment she'd been avoiding. The terrible poem their friend had posted. The weird way time felt lately. Stretching, collapsing, doing its own thing.

There were no big words. No promises made at midnight. Just two people, tired, honest, and still talking.

When the call finally settled, Aryan said, "We don't have to label anything. We just… don't stop."

Sara didn't answer. But she didn't end the call either.

She let the phone rest beside her pillow, screen facing down, and stayed there, breathing, listening, not pulling away.

The line eventually clicked off on its own.
But she didn't move.

CHAPTER 14

The Question He Couldn't Keep In

*Sometimes the hardest part isn't liking someone.
It's admitting what the liking demands.*

Two weeks had passed, not in silence, but in that strange, polite distance people use when they're trying not to cause damage.

They still spoke, but the warmth had thinned. Nothing sudden. Nothing explosive. Just a simple change, like the air between them had cooled without either of them meaning to.

Sara needed space. She never said it outright, but she pulled back in small, unmistakable ways, shorter replies, longer gaps, less ease. She wasn't punishing him. She was sorting herself out, and she didn't know how to do it with him watching.

Aryan didn't chase. Not because he didn't care, but because he sensed she needed the room. Still, the distance didn't sit lightly on him. You can respect someone's silence and still worry about everything living inside it.

One late evening, he gave up pretending he was busy. His laptop had been open for nearly an hour, blank screen burning white. He wasn't writing. He hadn't been able to for days. His mind kept circling the same thought:

This isn't going away on its own.

So, he picked up his phone.

Nothing rehearsed. Just the truth typed plainly.

Aryan: Hi, Sara. Hope you're okay. Can we talk?

He didn't mean "big talk." He meant real talk. But he knew she'd hear the weight in it.

Her reply came soon.

Sara: Talk? You're sounding very serious. What's happening?

Even through text, he could feel her trying to soften it, trying to keep the moment from turning sharp.

Aryan: Thanks for responding.

Sara: Why do you sound like you're emailing me? Just say it.

He stared at the screen for a few seconds. Then he stopped pretending he didn't already know what he wanted to ask.

Aryan: Do you like me, Sara? Or did I imagine everything between us?

The question landed exactly where she'd been avoiding looking.

She put her phone down for a moment. Exhaled once. She wasn't shocked. She had known they'd reach this point. She just hoped she could delay it until she felt stronger.

Finally, she typed:

Sara: I do like you. That part isn't confusing.
But that's not the problem I'm stuck with.

He read it twice, jaw tightening, not with anger, but with a kind of tired relief. She wasn't denying anything.

Aryan: Then what is the problem?

She didn't wrap it in poetry. She didn't sugarcoat.

Sara: You're consistent. You're sure.

You know how to show up.
I don't know if I can match that. Not now.

Her message hit him with the weight of honesty, not
rejection.

Aryan: Why not try? Why not give us a chance instead
of deciding the ending before we even begin?

This time, she took longer.

Not because she didn't know what to say.
Because she was forcing herself to be brave enough to
say it.

Sara: Because I'm scared. I'll let you down.
Not on purpose. Just because I'm not… stable enough
yet.

He leaned back, rubbing his forehead with his thumb.
She wasn't wrong. She was naming the exact fear that
had been vibrating in the space between them.

Aryan: Do you trust me at least?

Sara: I trust you. But I don't trust myself.
Sometimes I retreat without warning. Sometimes I shut
down even when I don't want to.
And I don't want you to carry the weight of that.

His chest tightened.

Not from hurt, from understanding too much.

Aryan: I'm not asking you to be perfect. I'm asking you not to vanish.
Let me stand with you. That's it.

A long pause.

Then she wrote:

Sara: It's always you reaching.
And me feeling like I'm behind.
How long until that exhausts you?

He closed his eyes. He knew the answer instantly.

Aryan: I'd rather try and stumble than watch something real fade because we were both too scared to name it.

She felt that line. Not because it was romantic, but because it was honest.
He wasn't chasing a fantasy.
He was asking for effort, not guarantees.

Then she asked the hardest question of the night.

Sara: Why don't you just let me go?
It would be easier for you.

He felt a cold shock in his chest. Not anger, fear.
Because she truly meant it.

Because she thought she was doing him a favour.

He sat up straighter, thumbs already typing.

Aryan: Because I'd regret walking away.
Not trying would eat at me more than falling short ever
could.

She read it, and for a moment, something unguarded
cracked open inside her.

Sara: I'm afraid, Aryan.
Afraid of messing this up.
Afraid of hurting you while I'm still figuring myself out.

He answered without delay.

Aryan: I'm not here to force anything.
I'm here because I see something worth building.
Even if it scares you. Even if it's slow.

The silence that followed wasn't cold or heavy.
It felt like both of them finally letting the truth breathe.

A few minutes later, she wrote:

Sara: I hear you.
I just… don't know how to walk into something that
might break me.

Aryan: Then walk slowly. I'm not going anywhere.

Another small pause.

Then:

Sara: Goodnight, Aryan.
Thank you for not making me feel like I disappear when I'm scared.

He exhaled, something soft but calm settling in his chest.
Not victory. Not certainty.
Just an honest beginning.

Aryan: Goodnight, Sara.
Take your time. I'm here.

It wasn't a promise.
But it was enough for now.

Nothing was resolved that night.
But they finally said the things that kept bruising the
silence.
Sometimes that's the only way a story keeps going.

CHAPTER 15

The Night He Showed Up

Some nights you don't plan. You just go.

It started like a dull evening. The kind where the room looks the same as it did yesterday, and the next thing you notice is how loud the clock seems when you're not doing anything to drown it out.

Aryan's desk was a mess, half-scribbled notes, an open water bottle he never finished, a charger hanging off the edge. The room felt like a paused life. The kind where you know something is waiting outside the door, but you haven't moved yet.

He looked at the time. 10:45 p.m. The number felt larger than the numbers usually do.

There was no plan. There was a pull, stupid, physical, like an itch under the ribs that refused to go away. He stood up, grabbed his jacket, and shoved his phone into his pocket. Before he could think it over and talk himself out of it, he texted his friend.

"Come with me. No questions. Need backup."

The response came fast.
"What madness are you manufacturing now?"

"Just come."

"Fine. This better be worth my sleep."

The city at that hour had a softness to it, less traffic, neon signs blinking in patterns. There's a particular kind of silence that follows when you're too aligned with a decision to doubt it. His focus was elsewhere. Fixed. Centered.

They drove with that late-night silence that makes every street seem private. His friend kept joking to break the tension.

"Yo," his friend called over the wind. "You sure about this?"

Aryan tightened his grip on the handlebars. "If you're sure about something, is it even worth doing?"

His friend groaned. "You're either a romantic genius or an absolute idiot."

"Probably both."

They parked a block away.

"Do I get to see the magic trick?" he asked.

"Not magic," Aryan said. "Just the honest thing."

His friend clapped him on the shoulder. "Go get it, then. If you screw this up, I'll never let you forget."

The street outside Sara's house rested in a charged silence, the kind that almost dared him to disturb it. Moonlight didn't matter. Trees didn't matter.

The world had narrowed itself to this singular purpose.

He pulled out his phone and typed, not because he needed to negotiate this with her, but because he wanted the ridiculous confirmation that she was still the person who would notice a late-night text.

"Did your uncle wish you yet?"

Her reply came faster than he expected.

"He did. Why?"

"Good. Because now it's my turn. Step outside."

Silence. Then a single, disbelieving message: "Are you joking?"

He sent a photograph of the lamp, the one that lit his face and made his eyes look like two dark coins.

The response came faster this time. "What the hell? Aryan! Don't move. I'm coming."

He didn't. He waited. He felt absurd and courageous at the same time, like a person standing under a small, clear light, daring something that might be tiny but mattered.

Inside her house, Sara was still dressed in the clothes she'd worn to dinner: a simple dress that fit like it had in other, ordinary nights. Her grandparents had wished her and gone to bed. She'd smiled, hugged people, wrapped little plates, the motions of family around a small celebration.

She had expected the night to end in peace and sleep. Instead, the message hit her like a spark.

She should have rolled her eyes. She should have typed back something sharp. She should have stayed inside and been sensible. Instead, her legs moved before her brain finished deciding.

The window opened with a familiar hiss. She climbed down the drainpipe like she had once when she was younger and had less sense of what could go wrong.

Her feet hit the ground sooner than she thought, and for a brief second, she laughed, not loud, not funny, just the noise of surprise at herself. She wasn't stealthy. She wasn't trying to be secretive. She just wanted to be there.

He saw her before she saw him.

A silhouette framed by the streetlight, hair slightly unkempt, breath making small clouds in the cool air, expression somewhere between disbelief and wonder.

She reached him, cheeks puffed, a half-smile on her face. "You're insane."

"Good insane or bad insane?" he asked immediately, because old habits die hard.

She considered. "Maybe both."

He shrugged, the kind of shrug that said, I know this is ridiculous, but I had to try anyway.

He didn't have roses. He didn't have a playlist or a banner or any Instagram-ready prop. He had his hands in his pockets and his friend parked a respectful distance behind them, pretending to be neutral but clearly delighted.

"You came," she said, voice not surprised, but softened.

"I didn't bring anything," he admitted. "No gift. Nothing smart to say."

"Why'd you come then?"

He shrugged, almost smiling. "To see you. Just that."

"You remembered."

"Of course I did."

She looked at him the way people look when they're checking whether what they hoped for is actually there. Not searching for performance, but proof. She reached up and smoothed a strand of hair away from her face, the small, ordinary gesture of someone who's still learning what it means not to be guarded all the time.

A car passed by, headlights sweeping over them.

Sara froze. "Is that—?"

Aryan reached out, touched her wrist lightly. "Relax. It's not your uncle. Text your cousin and check."

She fumbled for her phone, typing fast. A moment later, she sighed in relief. "You're right. It wasn't him."

"Told you."

The tension dissolved.
But Aryan didn't move his hand.
And Sara didn't pull away.

She reached the door of her car, opened it, and slid inside.

He leaned against the door, close, the body language of two people who didn't need words for a while.

There was a silence, not empty, but full of whatever they hadn't managed to say in polite conversation and late texts.

And then—

He kissed her.

It began tentative, the sort of first contact that asks permission with its gentleness.

Her fingers found the edge of his jacket, and he felt the small, sharp tug of relief that happened when someone returns the risk.

The kiss deepened a half-beat later, not because someone shouted action, but because both of them let go a little.

When he finally pulled back, she just stared at him. Lips parted. Eyes wide.

It wasn't with surprise or apology.

It was with breath.

"You…" she said, still breathless. "You're impossible."

Aryan smirked. "Anytime for you."

"You don't make sense," she said.

"Neither does half the world," he replied.

They laughed, small and embarrassed, then serious in the same breath. His friend called from down the street in a voice that read as mock-impatience. "You two done plotting my career's early retirement yet?"

"Shut up," Aryan called back, but he was laughing too.

After he reached home, Aryan saw her message.

**"You really have no idea how happy I was tonight.
I've never done something this crazy before.
But with you…it didn't feel crazy.
It felt like meeting myself again.
Thank you for making me feel seen."**

He read it in his room like a small physical thing, something you could put in your pocket.

Then he typed:
"Thank you for being worth the madness. Sleep well."

They didn't make plans. They didn't promise forever. They did something better: they showed up, awkward and imperfect, and let the night stand for what it was, a real step forward and not a performance.

When Aryan finally unplugged his phone and set it on the table, the glow dimmed, but he felt lighter, not because the problem was solved but because he'd stopped researching ways to avoid the thing that scared him. He'd done something physical about it. He'd been ridiculous and brave and human.

Two calls. One ride. One kiss. A single message that felt like arrival.

It wasn't perfect. It didn't need to be. It was practical, messy, honest. It moved things forward in a way that words on their own rarely do. And for the first time in a while, the future felt slightly less like a question and more like a direction.

Not every gesture changes a life. But some do change the way you walk toward it. This night didn't fix them. It started the work.

CHAPTER 16

The Night Things Changed

Two people can want the same thing and still be terrified of it.

It was a morning that didn't announce itself.

No golden sunlight slipping through curtains, no sudden change in atmosphere. Just an ordinary day beginning the way most days do, slow, balanced, indifferent to whatever happened the night before.

But something stayed, small, not loud. The kind of change you feel more than understand. A balance. An endurance. The kind that disappears if you stare at it too directly.

Sara's home stood with the calm of something that didn't need to impress anyone. It wasn't curated or aesthetic, it just existed. And Aryan, standing at the gate, felt the silence not as distance, but as permission.

"Come in," she said, leaning lightly against the doorway. The tone was casual, but something underneath it carried weight.

He stepped inside. The hallway was narrow, familiar. Old wooden shelves, small framed memories, small lived-in chaos. Nothing looked expensive, but everything had been kept, intentionally or stubbornly.

He paused at the photographs on the wall. Versions of her he'd never met, carefree, laughing, sun-warmed. But the arrangement was precise. Not a display, more like a guarded archive.

They moved room to room without plan, his eyes absorbing, hers softly allowing. At her bedroom doorway, she hesitated, not dramatically, just a small pause like checking with herself.

"This is it," she said, with a shrug that was almost a defense. "My empire of borrowed mornings and half-meant beginnings."

The room wasn't messy, but it wasn't tidy either. A bed made too neatly. A desk with papers stacked more emotionally than logically. A kitchenette that clearly worked harder than the rest of the room. Suitcases leaned against a wall, not temporary, just never fully unpacked.

"You weren't exaggerating about storage," Aryan murmured.

She smirked, not playful, not embarrassed, just honest. "Sentimentalism disguised as practicality. Or maybe…I'm still unpacking parts of myself I don't fully understand."

He didn't respond right away. Sometimes silence is the right form of listening.

"Do they all have a story?" he asked eventually.

"Some," she said. "Others are just… pieces of time. You think you've moved on from them, but somehow, they keep traveling with you."

The silence after that wasn't heavy. It was full.

THE KITCHEN

Sara moved to the tiny kitchenette. She didn't measure anything, just moved with muscle memory. Boil water. Spoon coffee. Stir. Breathe.

"This setup," she said, tapping the counter lightly, "has been everything. My hearth, my battlefield. My sanity."

Aryan leaned beside her. "You built all of this."

She nodded once, then corrected him, not sharply, just honestly:

"I built it because there wasn't anyone else to."

The coffee kettle clicked. The sound broke whatever softness was forming, and also made space for the next truth.

He asked gently, "Are you okay?"

She didn't answer immediately. She kept stirring her coffee long after it had dissolved.

"I'm functioning," she finally said.

"That's not what I asked."

She leaned back against the counter, holding her mug like it was grounding her.

"Do you ever miss someone," she asked, "not because of what they said or did, but because of the way life felt when they were in it?"

Aryan's jaw tightened, not with struggle, but recognition.

"Yes," he said. "Sometimes it's not even missing anymore, it's just a constant presence."

She nodded slowly.

"My father was like that."

THE WEIGHT SHE KEPT SILENT

She spoke without dramatizing anything.

"He died when I was young. One of those illnesses that doesn't negotiate, it just takes."

She kept her eyes on the mug, not him.

"When he was gone, everything changed. Not suddenly, more like the floor giving way one plank at a time."

Aryan didn't interrupt. Sometimes the most respectful thing is staying silent.

"My mother got married again. She called it moving on. I called it forgetting."

Her tone wasn't bitter. Just tired in a way that didn't need sympathy.

"I didn't fight it. I just stopped fitting. And when you don't fit anymore, people either reshape you or push you out. So, I left before either could happen."

She took a breath.

"My uncle, he took me in. The only person who didn't try to rewrite me."

The room felt different after that. Not tragic, just true.

"You built your life from pieces no one else wanted," he said gently.

"No," she said. "I built it because no one else would."

THE CONNECTION BETWEEN THEM
Time passed without being acknowledged.

Aryan reached for her hand, not to fix anything, not to comfort, just to say I'm here.

"Thank you," he murmured.

She stared at their hands for a moment. "I wasn't planning to tell you any of this."

"Maybe it wasn't planned," he said. "Maybe it needed somewhere to land."

She huffed a small, unbelieving laugh. "You make everything sound like it's meant."

"No," he admitted. "Just the true things."

She didn't pull her hand back.

BEFORE HE LEAVES

They sat on the small balcony for a while. No deep conversations. No emotional highs. Just air. Just presence.

When he finally stood to leave, she walked him to the door.

"Thanks for coming," she said softly. Less guarded than before.

He held her gaze, not demanding, just present.

"You're not alone, Sara. Even when you think you are."

She swallowed. Not heavily, just because something in that sentence hit somewhere it wasn't used to being touched.

"Maybe I'll believe that someday."

"Until then," he said, "I'll keep showing up."

She smirked, soft, tired, real.

"If I forget, I'll invoice you. Your emotional support rates are terrible."

He laughed under his breath. "Add it to my debt."

She watched him walk away. Usually, she'd close the door fast, like ending the moment before it could ask anything of her.

This time, she let it stay open. Just a few seconds longer.

Not lighter.
Not healed.
Just… less alone.

And that was enough for that day.

They didn't figure everything out. But they stopped pretending nothing was happening. That was enough for now.

Chapter 17

When Someone Stays

Some people don't leave, even when you expect them to.

The corridor looked the same as always, same walls, same muted lights, but something between them had changed. The silence wasn't empty anymore. It had weight. Not pressure, just… presence.

A chair scraped somewhere behind them. A door shut. Someone laughed in the distance. Life carried on, but none of it entered their space.

Aryan and Sara walked slowly, not because they wanted to drag time, but because neither of them seemed ready to rush anything.

Sara adjusted the strap of her bag. A small habit. The kind people do when they don't know where to put their hands.

Aryan finally spoke, voice low, almost casual.

"Mind if we don't take the straight path today?"

She looked at him, not fully, just enough to gauge intention.

"No."

"Good. I've had enough of straight lines for a while."

It made her mouth twitch, not a smile, not yet, but close. They turned left instead of forward. No plan. Just space.

A minute passed before she spoke again, and the question seemed to fall out of her more than be chosen.

"Why do you keep showing up like this?"

Aryan didn't react with surprise. He kept walking.

"What do you mean?"

"The consistency. The calm. The way you…" she exhaled, frustrated with the unfinished sentence. "Never mind."

He didn't fill the silence. He waited.

"I don't think it's about doing," he said eventually. "It's about staying."

Sara swallowed, jaw tightening slightly. "You don't have to stay."

"I know."

"Then why do you?"

This time, he slowed, not completely stopping, just matching his pace to the thought forming.

"Because when something matters," he said in a calm voice, "you don't wait for it to get easy."

She looked away, not out of discomfort, but because looking straight at him made everything feel too real too fast.

After a moment she said, almost to herself, "I don't think I know how to do this kind of connection."

Aryan stopped walking. She stopped a second later.

"What kind?" he asked.

"This," she said, hands lifting slightly before falling again. "The kind that doesn't disappear when I'm messy. Silent. Hard to read."

He let out a small breath, not pity, not amusement, recognition.

"You think you're the only uneven one?"

She didn't answer.

"I wasn't looking for perfection," he said. "I wasn't even looking for someone who matches me. I just… came ready to learn you. At your pace."

That landed. She didn't soften, but something in her posture changed. Less guarded, maybe.

"I don't need you to perform," he added. "Just be real."

Sara's fingers tightened on her bag strap again, habit, shield, translation.

They started walking once more.

A few steps later she asked, softer but more certain, "You could be anywhere. Why here?"

He almost smiled. "I've asked myself that."

"And?"

"I don't know if there's a clean answer," he said. "Maybe I just feel something here that makes silence feel like… a conversation."

She huffed, not annoyed, just slightly overwhelmed.

"That's still not an answer."

He chuckled. "Then maybe I just know. And that's enough."

Before she could reply, someone called her name.

"Sara!"

She turned, face falling back into its usual composed expression in a heartbeat. A classmate waved, asked something quick. Sara nodded.

"I'll be there in ten."

The girl offered Aryan a polite smile before leaving.

Aryan raised a brow. "Popular."

Sara rolled her eyes, but the edge was gone. "Temporary."

He lifted his shoulders, hands in his pockets. "Everything is."

They reached the courtyard, silent, usually ignored. A stone bench waited under a worn tree. Aryan paused.

"Sit?"

She nodded.

They sat, not too close, not distant. Just enough.

For a moment, nothing moved except the breeze tugging a loose strand of her hair. She brushed it away absently.

Aryan rested his hands on his knees, fingers laced. No rehearsed tone, no grand delivery, just truth.

"I don't know where this goes," he said. "But I'll keep showing up."

She looked at him, really looked, not through him or around him.

"Even when I don't make it easy?"

"Especially then."

Her eyes lowered, not from doubt, but because belief feels heavier than fear at first.

He added softly, almost like an afterthought,
"You don't have to earn space with me. You already have it."

Something eased in her. Not solved. Not fixed.
Just eased.

They didn't speak again for a while.

And for the first time, silence didn't feel like a test.

It felt like a beginning.

CHAPTER 18

A Year Without Answers

*If something stays without being held,
maybe it's worth keeping.*

Some changes don't arrive loudly. They creep in. Silent. Familiar. Almost mistaken for nothing.

Sara didn't wake up with certainty, but she woke up without fear.

That was new.

There was no clear answer, no big talk. Just an exhausted kind of acceptance: she wasn't running anymore. Not toward him. Not away from him.
Just… staying long enough to see the truth.

The evening carried the remains of last night, not memory, but atmosphere.
Her own voice still carried in patches through her mind:
What are we? What are we not? Why does naming feel like trapping?

She stood at the roadside waiting, arms crossed, jacket loose around her shoulders, weight shifting heel to toe. The banyan tree behind her felt older than every question they'd ever avoid. A motorbike rattled past, then a truck rolled by, its headlights sweeping briefly over her face before everything went dim again.

No metaphor.
No cinematic glow.
Just a girl waiting, but not waiting helplessly.

She wasn't hoping he would show, she just knew he would.

And then, gravel sound, even footsteps.

Sara didn't turn right away; her body already knew it was him.

Aryan walked toward her, denim jacket over one shoulder, posture relaxed, but his eyes searching her like he was checking for cracks.

"You've been here long?" he asked, casual voice, careful gaze.

"Not really," she said. "I needed the time anyway."

That answer landed heavier than she intended.

Aryan folded his jacket and leaned against the tree. Not touching her. Not stepping too close. Just being there, in a way that said: I'm not rushing you.

Sara inhaled, exhaled, then finally said the thing she'd rehearsed and un-rehearsed a dozen times:

"Let's give this a year."

Aryan didn't respond immediately, not because he didn't understand, but because he wanted to hear the rest before forming a reaction.

"A year without labels," she continued. "No pressure. No roles. No pretending we know where this is going."

His brow lifted slightly.

"A year," he repeated, not sarcastic, not doubtful, just absorbing.

Sara kept speaking, slower this time:

"I don't want to declare something we haven't lived. I don't want us calling it love just because the timing feels convenient. If it becomes something real, it will survive not being named."

Aryan studied her. Not defensive. Not annoyed. Just present.

"You're asking for… space," he said.

"No," she corrected. "I'm asking for truth. Without shortcuts."

He nodded once, slow.

Then he asked the question she knew was coming:

"And what if, somewhere in that year, we lose each other?"

Sara didn't pause.

"Then we were never meant to stay," she said softly.

That answer stung him, she saw it, but he didn't push back. He just swallowed, adjusted his grip on the jacket, and let the honesty settle.

The silence wasn't uncomfortable. It was… adult. Necessary. The kind where two people stop romanticizing what they want and start respecting what's real.

Aryan finally said:

"You know, most people don't ask for honesty like this. They ask for certainty."

Sara smiled, not soft, not mocking, just tired.

"I've lived certainty," she said. "It was full of assumptions and fear. I want something built slowly. Something that doesn't collapse when life turns."

He let out a small breath, half disbelief, half admiration.

"You make this harder and easier at the same time."

"I know," she said.

Another small beat.

Then he smirked slightly, loosening the weight of the moment.

"So, in this arrangement... am I still allowed to steal your time?"

"You can try," she said, raising an eyebrow. "Just don't expect privileges you haven't earned."

"That sounded cryptic."

"No," she replied, "just boundaries."

He laughed under his breath and then, with a little boyish stubbornness, he nudged her shoulder.

"Say it once."

She blinked. "Say what?"

"You know," he said, eyes narrowing with exaggerated expectation. "The forbidden line."

Sara exhaled, pretending to be annoyed, but something softened in her.

She didn't say it dramatically. Didn't romanticize it.

She just said it the way truth should be said, plainly:

"I love you."

Aryan didn't move closer. Didn't tease. Didn't grin.

He just held the moment.

"Thank you," he said in a calm voice. "I'll take care of that."

Not I love you too.
Not finally.
Just a promise to not treat it lightly.

No kiss followed, because kissing would've made it performative.
Instead, the air between them warmed, even, alive.

After a while, he spoke again:

"I'm leaving tomorrow."

Sara nodded. She already knew.

"Back home?"

"Yeah. Just for a little while. But don't worry, I'll be back soon. Can't let you off the hook that easily."

She didn't ask how long. She didn't ask what it meant.

"Take what you need," she said softly. "Just don't forget where you were growing."

He looked at her then, really looked, with something between respect and yearning.

She reached up, hand brushing his cheek briefly. Not a claim. Not reassurance. Just remembrance.

Then she stepped away and opened the car door.

Aryan leaned down to the window with a half-smirk.

"You still owe me something."

Sara held his gaze.

"Then earn it," she said. "Next time."

She drove off.

He didn't wave.
He didn't chase.
He just stood there, watching the taillights disappear,
feeling not abandoned, not heartbroken, but ready.

Not for certainty.
For whatever comes.

CHAPTER 19

She Didn't Walk Away This Time

People don't change all at once.
Sometimes, the only progress is staying instead of leaving.

The day after saying goodbye always feels slower than it should.

Last night, before they disconnected, Aryan had told Sara, "I'll be leaving tomorrow morning."
She didn't say much, but something in her voice tightened. Not enough to call it sadness. Just enough to call it real.

Morning came with travel, not thought. Vehicles, roads, checkpoints, the passing blur of movement that didn't match what his mind was doing, replaying conversation pieces and looks that stayed longer than words.

By the time he reached home, evening had already settled. He barely managed to pull off his shoes before exhaustion hit. His body gave up on the couch, no blanket, no intention, just gravity and silence. The kind that comes after emotional weight, not physical effort.

When he finally got up, the room looked unfamiliar in the dim light. The curtains let in just enough streetlamp glow to form silhouettes. The clock on his phone read 11:42 PM.

He blinked twice, breathing even but heavy, the kind of heaviness that isn't sadness, just fullness.

His phone was under his palm, warm from being held earlier. When he unlocked it, her name was there.

Sara.

A notification sitting silent, not demanding anything, just waiting.

He tapped it.

"Have you reached home safely?"

Simple. Ordinary. But something about it tightened his chest, not painfully, just noticeably.

Because the message wasn't about location.
It was about presence.

He exhaled through his nose, thumb hovering before he typed:

"Sorry, I passed out. Long day. But yeah, home safe."

He wasn't expecting a fast reply.

But it came almost immediately.

"Well, I'm dead tired too. Maybe you can put me in the right mood."

He stared at the message a second longer than necessary.

Not flirtation. Not hinting.
Just honest exhaustion where softness leaked out without permission.

He let a small half-smile appear, nothing big, nothing grand, just the involuntary kind that comes when someone gets close without trying.

He typed:

"One lovable message from you could change my mood too, you know."

He sent it casually.
Meant every word.

This time, her reply didn't come immediately.
He could almost picture her holding the phone, rereading, deciding whether to respond lightly or truthfully.

When it came, it wasn't playful anymore.

"I wish I could. I've thought about it so many times, Aryan. But something holds me back."

His posture changed, shoulders pulling back, jaw relaxing, breathing slower.

Something had changed.

He typed:

"What holds you back? My terrible jokes? Or my habit of oversharing?"

A laughing emoji arrived, her usual way of softening serious things before they grew teeth.

Then another message:

"No, it's me. I'm… scared, Aryan. If I become too expressive, I feel like I'll become emotionally weak. And I can't afford to be that again."

He leaned back on the couch, eyes closed, not overwhelmed, just absorbing.

Not because she was vulnerable.

But because she was honest.
Finally.

He typed slowly:

"You're not weak. You're forged. That's different. And it doesn't cancel out the parts of you that feel deeply."

He paused before sending it.
No edits. No polishing. He sent it as-is.

There was silence, not uncomfortable, just… processing.

Then:

"You've been patient with me. I know I'm difficult. I know I retreat. But I wasn't always like this. I used to open easily. And every time, it—"

She didn't finish the sentence.

She didn't have to.

He replied:

"I know. And I'm not leaving just because there are locked doors."

No hero tone.
No savior tone.
Just truth.

Another pause.
Longer.

Then:

"You really mean that?"

His thumbs moved without hesitation.

"I've never climbed so surely toward someone's truth before."

A heartbeat later, she sent:

"Twice."

He frowned slightly.

"Twice what?"

Her reply:

"Twice, I've wanted to tell you I love you. But I couldn't."

No background score.

No grand swell.

Just a real sentence landing where it needed to.

He didn't rush.
He didn't panic.

He sat with it, calm, grounded.

Then:

"Maybe next time, don't stop yourself."

Not pressure.
Just permission.

Her reply:

"Maybe."

A word with a pulse.

The tone between them softened, not because the serious part ended, but because they had already crossed it.

She teased him again.
He called her stubborn again.

Not flirtation, just familiar.

Then Aryan typed the question that had been sitting with him longer than he admitted:

"Can I ask you something?"

Her reply was quick.

"Of course."

He typed:

"Have you ever felt the urge to just… show love to me? Like actually show it?"

Not romantic pressure.
Not insecurity.
Just curiosity with breath behind it.

Her response took time.

Enough time for him to mentally prepare for either answer.

Then:

"Twice. Don't ask me when. I wouldn't know how to explain it."

He typed:

"Maybe you should've."

She replied:

"Maybe. Or maybe not."

He tried again, not pushing, just gently:

"And now?"

This time, the pause was long enough he placed the phone on his chest and stared at the ceiling.

When it came, it was soft.

"Now… it feels nice. Knowing I matter to someone."

He swallowed, slow, steady.

Then typed:

"You do. More than you've let yourself believe."

No exaggeration.
No add-ons.

Just truth.

Her final message:

"Goodnight, Aryan."

He stared at the word night long enough for it to say more than she ever would.

He replied:

"Goodnight, Sara."

He placed the phone facedown beside him.

Sleep didn't arrive fast.
Not because he was restless, because something had finally settled differently.

Not closure.
Not confession.

Just understanding.

The kind that doesn't demand a next step.

The kind that simply changes the air.

Maybe by morning everything would go back to the way it was.

Or maybe something gentle and undeniable had already changed, something neither of them could undo or rush.

For the first time in weeks, Aryan didn't feel like he was waiting.

She didn't walk away.

And for now—
that was enough.

Not everything ends with a choice.
Sometimes things just stop moving for a minute, not because the story is confused, but because the moment isn't done.

Tonight, didn't give them answers.
It gave them honesty.
And sometimes that's the thing that turns everything gently.

This wasn't a surrender.
It wasn't closure.
It was two people finally stopping long enough to feel what was actually happening.

Whatever comes next will grow from here, slow, unsure, but real.

CLOSING BREATH OF VOLUME ONE:

Gaze of Grace – A Door Without Keys

There's no neat ending waiting here.
No label.
No polished final scene.

They're not together.
They're not apart.
They're somewhere in the middle, trying to understand
themselves and each other without rushing the shape
of whatever this is becoming.

This volume wasn't about love arriving.
It was about the groundwork: the bruises, the fear, the
hesitation, the patience, the truths.
Two people unlearning their defenses long enough to
realize they don't have to run anymore.

No big declarations were spoken.
But something opened.

Sara isn't hiding behind distance.
Aryan isn't filling silence with assumptions.
They're standing in the same emotional room now,
not fully ready, not fully clear, but present.

The connection is there.
It's real.
It's unfinished.

Volume Two won't start with certainty, it'll start with the reality of two people who finally know there's something worth risking.

For now, this pause is the ending.

A breath held.
A door half open.
A story that's just starting to form its shape.

AUTHOR NOTE:

Thank you for reading, not just the moments, but the silence around them.
Not just the sentences, but the weight beneath them.

This book wasn't meant to rush toward a perfect ending. It was meant to follow two imperfect people who are trying to grow without pretending they're fearless or ready.

If you're someone who's figuring out how to stay, how to trust, how to show up even when something scares you, then maybe this ending makes sense to you.

It doesn't stop here because it's finished.

It stops here because the foundation's finally solid enough for what comes next.

See you in **Volume Two.**
Where things won't be easier, just truer.